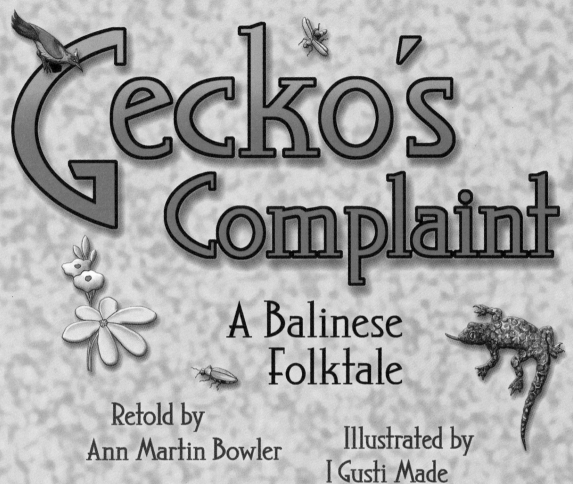

Gecko's Complaint

A Balinese Folktale

Retold by
Ann Martin Bowler

Illustrated by
I Gusti Made
Sukanada

PERIPLUS

Published by Periplus Editions (HK) Ltd.
Copyright © 2003 Ann Martin Bowler
Illustrated by I Gusti Made Sukanada
Book design by TLC Graphics, www.TLCGraphics.com

ISBN 0-7946-0165-0

Printed in Singapore

08 07 06 05 04   10 9 8 7 6 5 4 3 2

DISTRIBUTED BY:
Asia-Pacific
Berkeley Books Pte Ltd
130 Joo Seng Road, #06-01/03
Singapore 368357
Tel: (65) 6280 1330
Fax: (65) 6280 6290
Email: inquiries@periplus.com.sg

Japan
Tuttle Publishing
Yaekari Building 3F
5-4-12 Osaki, Shinagawa-ku
Tokyo 141-0032, Japan
Tel: (03) 5437 0171
Fax: (03) 5437 0755
Email: tuttle-sales@gol.com

North America, Latin America & Europe
Tuttle Publishing
364 Innovation Drive
North Clarendon, VT 05759-9436, USA
Tel: (802) 773 8930
Fax: (802) 773 6993
Email: info@tuttlepublishing.com
www.tuttlepublishing.com

Indonesia
PT Java Books Indonesia
Jl. Kelapa Gading Kirana
Blok A14 No. 17
Jakarta 14240. Indonesia
Tel: (62-21) 451 5351
Fax: (62-21) 453 4987
Email: cs@javabooks.co.id

DEDICATIONS

To Jocean, who brought Indonesia home to us.
Thank you!
AMB

To Mayun.
IGMS

An enormous gecko once lived on the island we now call Bali, in a jungle dense with flowers and vines. Gecko's jungle had so many insects he hardly had to move to find his supper. When a mosquito buzzed by his banyan tree, he just flicked out his long, sticky tongue and caught his dinner.

Gecko could do things the other animals only wished they could do. He could run up trees and across branches, hanging on by the tiny hooks on the end of his toes. If he lost his tail, he would grow a new one, stronger than the last. Gecko loved to prowl about at night. His loud call, "Geck-o, geck-o," woke the jungle animals from their sound sleep. They considered him a careless, self-centered fellow.

However, Gecko had his reasons. Sometimes Woodpecker drummed on his tree all through the night, keeping Gecko awake. Other times, just as he was dozing off, fireflies would gather in great numbers. They would fly around him, lighting up the evening sky, their red and yellow spots glowing like sparks of fire.

One evening, the fireflies gathered around Gecko's banyan tree. It began with one single, small flicker. The rest of the fireflies flashed in response, sending waves of light up and down the jungle. Their sparks were so bright, they seemed to change night into day. The fireflies flashed on, hour after hour, until Gecko could take it no more. "Geck-o, geck-o, geck-o!" he called, wearily trudging up the hill to consult Raden, the jungle's chief.

"This had better be important!" said Chief Raden, dragging himself out of bed. "It's the middle of the night."

"Oh, it is important, Chief," Gecko replied hastily. "I can't sleep! The fireflies keep flashing their lights."

The lion smiled. "Well, we seem to have the same problem. The fireflies disturb you and you disturb me."

"Yes," said Gecko, feeling ashamed. "I wouldn't complain, sir, but I just can't sleep!"

"I'll look into it," Raden promised.

Early the next morning, the lion paid a visit to the fireflies, asking, "Why do you bother others? Night is to be a peaceful, quiet time in our jungle."

The fireflies answered meekly. "We meant no harm by our flashing! Woodpecker was drumming all night, sending signals of alarm. We were just passing his message on."

Raden had no trouble finding Woodpecker. His loud hammering echoed far and wide. "Please explain your endless tapping!" demanded the lion.

Woodpecker explained quickly, "Black Beetle leaves manure all over the jungle path. She must be stopped before we all get sick from this filthy dung! I've been tapping to warn the others."

"This is a serious matter!" Raden agreed. "I will find Beetle immediately."

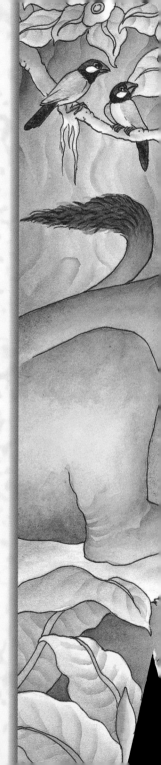

Black Beetle, plump and gleaming like polished copper, was busy rolling her filthy loads when Chief Raden arrived. Beetle stopped working and humbly explained, "Water Buffalo strolls down the path often, sir, and drops his patties of manure as he walks. I'm only doing my duty by cleaning the pathway."

Raden, worn out by all the complaining, set out for home. Before leaving, he instructed Black Beetle, "Send Water Buffalo to me the moment you see him!"

Water Buffalo rushed to Chief Raden's home, ready to defend himself. "No one understands my work! Rain makes huge potholes in the jungle path. I leave my dung on the pathway to fill up these holes, making it easier for all to travel."

The lion let out a roar that shook the jungle. Weary from the endless complaints, yet unwilling to give up, Raden decided to speak directly to Rain. He set out for Gunung Batur, a tall mountain where Rain is always near.

20

Storm clouds gathered as the lion lumbered up the mountain. The blowing Wind made his climb difficult. When he reached Gunung Batur's highest peak, Chief Raden roared loudly. "Rain, why are you ruining the jungle pathways and causing so many problems for the animals?"

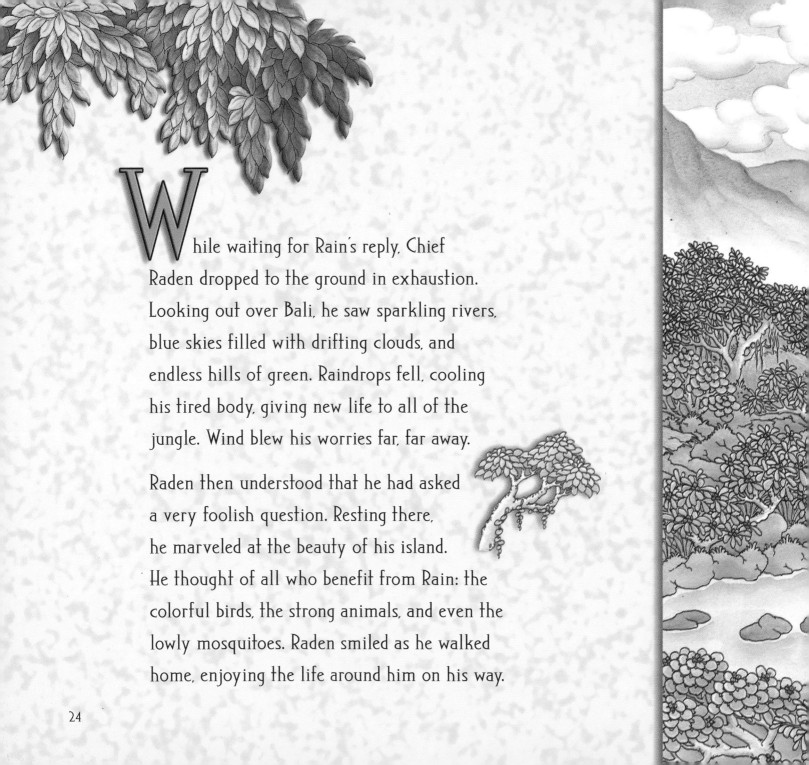

W hile waiting for Rain's reply, Chief Raden dropped to the ground in exhaustion. Looking out over Bali, he saw sparkling rivers, blue skies filled with drifting clouds, and endless hills of green. Raindrops fell, cooling his tired body, giving new life to all of the jungle. Wind blew his worries far, far away.

Raden then understood that he had asked a very foolish question. Resting there, he marveled at the beauty of his island. He thought of all who benefit from Rain: the colorful birds, the strong animals, and even the lowly mosquitoes. Raden smiled as he walked home, enjoying the life around him on his way.

W hen he arrived home, Chief Raden summoned Gecko and the other complaining animals. The Chief spoke sternly. "Think of the gifts that Rain gives to us: the rivers, the many plants of the jungle, and the food that we eat."

"And may I remind you, Gecko, that
without Rain, there would be no mosquitoes,
and without mosquitoes, you would be a
hungry and unhappy fellow."

In a powerful voice, Chief Raden commanded, "Quit your complaining! Go home and live in peace with one another!"

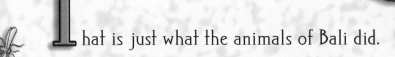

T hat is just what the animals of Bali did.

Today, Woodpecker is careful not to hammer
on Gecko's tree. The fireflies still light up
the evening sky, but not close to Gecko.
And Gecko, who grows fatter each day,
finds little to complain about.